'THE ILLEGIBLE
SIGNATURE OF
TEETERING
DISASTER...'

VLADIMIR NABOKOV
Born 1899, St Petersburg, Russia
Died 1977, Montreux, Switzerland

'The Aurelian' was written in Russian in 1931 and translated by Peter Pertzov in collaboration with the author; 'Signs and Symbols' was written in English in 1948 and 'Lance', Nabokov's last short story, in 1951. They are all included in *Nabokov's Dozen* and *Collected Stories*.

VLADIMIR NABOKOV

Lance

PENGUIN BOOKS

PENGUIN CLASSICS

UK | USA | Canada | Ireland | Australia
India | New Zealand | South Africa

Penguin Books is part of the Penguin Random House group
of companies whose addresses can be found at
global.penguinrandomhouse.com.

Penguin
Random House
UK

This selection first published 2018
003

Set in 11.2/13.75 pt Dante MT Std
Typeset by Jouve (UK), Milton Keynes
Printed and bound in Great Britain by Clays Ltd, Elcograf S.p.A.

ISBN: 978-0-241-33952-7

www.greenpenguin.co.uk

MIX
Paper from
responsible sources
FSC® C018179

Penguin Random House is committed to a
sustainable future for our business, our readers
and our planet. This book is made from Forest
Stewardship Council® certified paper.

Contents

The Aurelian

I

Luring aside one of the trolley-car numbers, the street started at the corner of a crowded avenue. For a long time it crept on in obscurity, with no shop windows or any such joys. Then came a small square (four benches, a bed of pansies) round which the trolley steered with rasping disapproval. Here the street changed its name, and a new life began. Along the right side, shops appeared: a fruiterer's, with vivid pyramids of oranges; a tobacconist's, with the picture of a voluptuous Turk; a delicatessen, with fat brown and grey coils of sausages; and then, all of a sudden, a butterfly store. At night, and especially when it was damp, with the asphalt shining like the back of a seal, passers-by would stop for a second before that symbol of fair weather. The insects on exhibit were huge and gorgeous. People would say to themselves, 'What colours – amazing!' and plod on through the drizzle. Eyed wings wide-open in wonder, shimmering blue satin, black magic – these lingered for a while floating in one's vision, until one boarded the trolley or bought a newspaper. And, just because they were together with the butterflies, a few other objects would remain in one's memory: a globe, pencils, and a monkey's skull on a pile of copybooks.

As the street blinked and ran on, there followed again a succession of ordinary shops – soap, coal, bread – with another pause at the corner where there was a small bar. The bartender, a dashing fellow in a starched collar and green sweater, was deft at shaving off with one stroke the foam topping the glass under the beer tap; he also had a well-earned reputation as a wit. Every night, at a round table by the window, the fruiterer, the baker, an unemployed man, and the bartender's first cousin played cards with great gusto. As the winner of the current stake immediately ordered four drinks, none of the players could ever get rich.

On Saturdays, at an adjacent table, there would sit a flabby elderly man with a florid face, lank hair, and a greyish moustache, carelessly clipped. When he appeared, the players greeted him noisily without looking up from their cards. He invariably ordered rum, filled his pipe, and gazed at the game with pink-rimmed watery eyes. The left eyelid drooped slightly.

Occasionally someone turned to him, and asked how

his shop was doing; he would be slow to answer, and often did not answer at all. If the bartender's daughter, a pretty freckled girl in a polka-dotted frock, happened to pass close enough, he had a go at her elusive hip, and, whether the slap succeeded or not, his gloomy expression never changed, although the veins on his temple grew purple. Mine host very humorously called him 'Herr Professor'. 'Well, how is the Herr Professor tonight?' he would ask, coming over to him, and the man would ponder for some time in silence and then, with a wet underlip pushing out from under the pipe like that of a feeding elephant, he would answer something neither funny nor polite. The bartender would counter briskly, which made the players at the next table, though seemingly absorbed in their cards, rock with glee.

The man wore a roomy grey suit with great exaggeration of the vest motif, and when the cuckoo popped out of the clock he ponderously extracted a thick silver watch and gazed at it askance, holding it in the palm of his hand and squinting because of the smoke. Punctually at eleven he knocked out his pipe, paid for his rum, and, after extending a flaccid hand to anyone who might choose to shake it, silently left.

He walked awkwardly, with a slight limp. His legs seemed too thin for his body. Just before the window of his shop he turned into a passage, where there was a door on the right with a brass plate: PAUL PILGRAM. This door led into his tiny dingy apartment, which could also be reached by an inner corridor at the back of the shop. Eleanor was usually asleep when he came home on those festive nights. Half a dozen faded photographs of the same clumsy ship, taken from different angles, and of a palm tree that looked as bleak as if it were growing on Heligoland hung in black frames above the double bed. Muttering to himself, Pilgram limped away into bulbless darkness with a lighted candle, came back with his braces dangling, and kept muttering while sitting on the edge of the bed and slowly, painfully, taking off his shoes. His wife, half-waking, moaned into her pillow and offered to help him; and then with a threatening rumble in his voice, he would tell her to keep quiet, and repeated that guttural *'Ruhe!'* several times, more and more fiercely.

After the stroke which had almost killed him some time ago (like a mountain falling upon him from behind just as he had bent towards his shoestrings), he now undressed reluctantly, growling until he got safely into bed, and then growling again if the tap happened to drip in the adjoining kitchen. Eleanor would roll out of bed and totter into the kitchen and totter back with a dazed sigh, her small face wax-pale and shiny, and the plastered corns on her feet showing from under her dismally long nightgown. They had married in 1905, almost a quarter of a century before, and were childless because Pilgram had always thought that children would be merely a hindrance to the realization of what had been in his youth a delightfully exciting plan but had now gradually become a dark, passionate obsession.

He slept on his back with an old-fashioned nightcap coming down on his forehead; it was to all appearances the solid and sonorous sleep that might be expected in an elderly German shopkeeper, and one could readily suppose that his quilted torpor was entirely devoid of visions; but actually this churlish, heavy man, who fed mainly on *Erbswurst* and boiled potatoes, placidly believing in his newspaper and quite ignorant of the world (in so far as his secret passion was not involved), dreamed of things that would have seemed utterly unintelligible to his wife or his neighbours; for Pilgram belonged, or rather was meant to belong (something – the place, the time, the man – had been ill-chosen), to a special breed of dreamers, such dreamers as used to be called in the old days 'Aurelians' – perhaps on account of those chrysalids, those 'jewels of nature', which they loved to find hanging on fences above the dusty nettles of country lanes.

On Sundays he drank his morning coffee in several sloppy sessions, and then went out for a walk with his wife, a slow silent stroll which Eleanor looked forward to all the week. On workdays he opened his shop as early as possible because of the children who passed by on their way to school; for lately he had been keeping school supplies in addition to his basic stock. Some small boy, swinging his satchel and chewing a sandwich, would slouch past the tobacconist's (where a certain brand of cigarettes offered aeroplane pictures), past the delicatessen (which rebuked one for having eaten that sandwich long before lunchtime), and then, remembering he wanted an eraser, would enter the next shop. Pilgram would mumble something, sticking out his lower lip from under the stem of his pipe, and, after a listless search, would plump down an open carton on the counter. The boy would feel and squeeze the virgin-pale India rubber, would not find the sort he favoured, and would leave without even noticing the principal wares in the store.

'These modern children!' Pilgram would think with disgust and he recalled his own boyhood. His father – a sailor, a rover, a bit of a rogue – married late in life a sallow-skinned, light-eyed Dutch girl whom he brought from Java to Berlin, and opened a shop of exotic curios. Pilgram could not remember now when, exactly, butterflies had began to oust the stuffed birds of paradise, the stale talismans, the fans with dragons, and the like; but as a boy he already feverishly swapped specimens with collectors, and after his parents died butterflies reigned supreme in the dim little shop. Up to 1914 there were enough amateurs and professionals about to keep things going in a mild, very mild, way; later on, however, it became necessary to make concessions, a display case with the biography of the silkworm furnishing a transition to school supplies just as in the old days pictures ignominiously composed of sparkling wings had probably been a first step towards lepidopterology.

Now the window contained, apart from penholders, mainly showy insects, popular stars among butterflies, some of them set on plaster and framed – intended merely for ornamenting the home. In the shop itself, permeated with the pungent odour of a disinfectant, the real, the precious collections were kept. The whole place was littered with various cases, cartons, cigar boxes. Tall cabinets contained numerous glass-lidded drawers filled with ordered series of perfect specimens impeccably spread and labelled. A dusty old shield or something (last remnant of the original wares) stood in a dark corner. Now and then live stock would appear: loaded brown pupae with a symmetrical confluence of delicate lines and grooves on the thorax, showing how the rudimentary wings, feet, antennae, and proboscis were packed. If one touched such a pupa as it lay on its bed of moss, the tapering end of the segmented abdomen would start jerking this way and that like the swathed limbs of a baby. The pupae cost a reichsmark apiece and in due time yielded a limp bedraggled, miraculously expanding moth. And sometimes other creatures would be temporarily on sale; just then there happened to be a dozen lizards, natives of Majorca, cold, black, blue-bellied things, which Pilgram fed on meal worms for the main course and grapes for dessert.

2

He had spent all his life in Berlin and its suburbs; had never travelled farther than Peacock Island on a neighbouring lake. He was a first-class entomologist. Dr Rebel, of Vienna, had named a certain rare moth *Agrotis pilgrami*; and Pilgram himself had published several descriptions. His boxes contained most of the countries of the world, but all he had ever seen of it was the dull sand-and-pine scenery of an occasional Sunday trip; and he would be reminded of captures that had seemed to him so miraculous in his boyhood as he melancholically gazed at the familiar fauna about him, limited by a familiar landscape, to which it corresponded as hopelessly as he to his street. From a roadside shrub he would pick up a large turquoise-green caterpillar with a china-blue horn on the last ring; there it lay quite stiff on the palm of his hand, and presently, with a sigh, he would put it back on its twig as if it were some dead trinket.

Although once or twice he had had the chance to switch to a more profitable business – selling cloth, for instance, instead of moths – he stubbornly held on to his shop as the symbolic link between his dreary existence and the phantom of perfect happiness. What he craved for, with a fierce, almost morbid intensity, was *himself* to net the rarest butterflies of distant countries, to see them in flight with his own eyes, to stand waist-deep in lush grass and feel the follow-through of the swishing net and then the furious throbbing of wings through a clutched fold of the gauze.

Every year it seemed to him stranger that the year before he had not managed somehow to lay aside enough money for at least a fortnight's collecting trip abroad, but he had never been thrifty, business had always been slack, there was always a gap somewhere, and, even if luck did come his way now and then, something was sure to go wrong at the last moment. He had married counting heavily on a share in his father-in-law's business, but a month later the man had died, leaving nothing but debts. Just before World War I an unexpected deal brought a journey to Algeria so near that he even acquired a sun helmet. When all travel stopped, he still consoled

9

himself with the hope that he might be sent to some exciting place as a soldier; but he was clumsy, sickly, not very young, and thus saw neither active service nor exotic Lepidoptera. Then, after the war, when he had managed again to save a little money (for a week in Zermatt, this time), the inflation suddenly turned his meagre hoard into something less than the price of a trolley-car ticket.

After that he gave up trying. He grew more and more depressed as his passion grew stronger. When some entomological acquaintance happened to drop in, Pilgram was only annoyed. 'That fellow,' he would think, 'may be as learned as the late Dr Staudinger, but he has no more imagination than a stamp collector.' The glass-lidded trays over which both were bending gradually took up the whole counter, and the pipe in Pilgram's sucking lips kept emitting a wistful squeak. Pensively he gazed at the serried rows of delicate insects all alike to you or me, and now and then he tapped on the glass with a stubby forefinger, stressing some special rarity. 'That's a curiously dark aberration,' the learned visitor might say. 'Eisner got one like that at an auction in London, but it was not so dark, and it cost him £14.' Painfully sniffling with his extinguished pipe, Pilgram would raise the box lid to the light, which made the shadows of the butterflies slip from beneath them across the papered bottom; then he would put it down again, and working in his nails under the tight edges of the lid, would shake it loose with a jerk and smoothly remove it. 'And Eisner's female was not so fresh,' the visitor would add, and some eavesdropper coming in for a copybook or a postage stamp might well wonder what on earth these two were talking about.

Grunting, Pilgram plucked at the gilded head of the black pin upon which the silky little creature was crucified, and took the specimen out of the box. Turning it this way and that, he peered at the label pinned under the body. 'Yes – Tatsienlu, East Tibet,' he read. 'Taken by the native collectors of Father Dejean' (which sounded almost like 'Prester John') – and he would stick the butterfly back again, right into the same pinhole. His motions seemed casual, even careless, but this was the unerring nonchalance of the specialist: the pin, with the precious insect, and Pilgram's fat fingers were the correlated parts of one and the same flawless machine. It might happen however, that some open box, having been brushed by the elbow of the visitor, would stealthily begin to slide off the counter – to be stopped just in the nick of time by Pilgram, who would then calmly go on lighting his pipe; only much later, when busy elsewhere, he would suddenly produce a moan of retrospective anguish.

★

But not only averted crashes made him moan. Father Dejean, stout-hearted missionary climbing among the rhododendrons and snows, how enviable was thy lot! And Pilgram would stare at his boxes and puff and brood and reflect that he need not go so far: that there were thousands of hunting grounds all over Europe. Out of localities cited in entomological works he had built up a special world of his own, to which his science was a most detailed guidebook. In that world there were no casinos, no old churches, nothing that might attract a normal tourist. Digne in southern France, Ragusa in Dalmatia, Sarepta on the Volga, Abisko in Lapland – those were the famous sites dear to butterfly collectors, and this is where they had poked about on and off, since the fifties of the last century (always greatly perplexing the local inhabitants). And as clearly as if it were a reminiscence Pilgram saw himself troubling the sleep of a little hotel by stamping and jumping about a room through the wide-open window of which, out of the black generous night, a whitish moth had dashed in and, in an audible bob dance, was kissing its shadow all over the ceiling.

In these impossible dreams of his he had visited the Islands of the Blessed, where in the hot ravines that cut the lower slopes of the chestnut- and laurel-clad mountains there occurs a weird local race of the cabbage white; and also that other island, those railway banks near

Vizzavona and the pine woods farther up, which are the haunts of the squat and dusky Corsican swallow-tail. He visited the far North, the Arctic bogs that produced such delicate downy butterflies. He knew the high Alpine pastures, with those flat stones lying here and there among the slippery matted grass; for there is no greater delight than to lift such a stone and find beneath it a plump sleepy moth of a still undescribed species. He saw glazed Apollo butterflies, ocellated with red, float in the mountain draught across the mule track that ran between a steep cliff and an abyss of wild white waters. In Italian gardens in the summer dusk, the gravel crunched invitingly underfoot, and Pilgram gazed through the growing darkness at clusters of blossoms in front of which suddenly there appeared an oleander hawk, which passed from flower to flower, humming intently and stopping at the corolla, its wings vibrating so rapidly that nothing but a ghostly nimbus was visible about its streamlined body. And best of all, perhaps, were the white heathered hills near Madrid, the valleys of Andalusia, fertile and wooded Albarracin, whither a little bus driven by the forest guard's brother groaned up a twisted road.

He had more difficulty in imagining the tropics, but experienced still keener pangs when he did, for never would he catch the loftily flapping Brazilian morphos, so ample and radiant that they cast an azure reflection upon one's hand, never come upon those crowds of African butterflies closely stuck like innumerable fancy flags into the rich black mud and rising in a coloured cloud when his shadow approached – a long, very long, shadow.

3

'Ja, ja, ja,' he would mutter, nodding his heavy head, and holding the case before him as if it were a beloved portrait. The bell over the door would tinkle, his wife would come in with a wet umbrella and a shopping bag, and slowly he would turn his back to her as he inserted the case into the cabinet. So it went on, that obsession and that despair and that nightmarish impossibility to swindle destiny, until a certain first of April, of all dates. For more than a year he had had in his keeping a cabinet devoted solely to the genus of those small clear-winged moths that mimic wasps or mosquitoes. The widow of a great authority on that particular group had given Pilgram her husband's collection to sell on commission. He hastened to tell the silly woman that he would not be able to get more than 75 marks for it, although he knew very well that, according to catalogue prices, it was worth fifty times more, so that the amateur to whom he would sell the lot for, say, a thousand marks would

consider it a good bargain. The amateur, however, did not appear, though Pilgram had written to all the wealthiest collectors. So he had locked up the cabinet, and stopped thinking about it.

That April morning a sunburned, bespectacled man in an old macintosh and without any hat on his brown bald head sauntered in, and asked for some carbon paper. Pilgram slipped the small coins paid for the sticky violet stuff he so hated to handle into the slit of a small clay money-pot, and, sucking on his pipe, fixed his stare into space. The man cast a rapid glance round the shop, and remarked upon the extravagant brilliancy of an iridescent green insect with many tails. Pilgram mumbled something about Madagascar. 'And that – that's not a butterfly, is it?' said the man, indicating another specimen. Pilgram slowly replied that he had a whole collection of that special kind. *'Ach was!'* said the man. Pilgram scratched his bristly chin, and limped into the recess of the shop. He pulled out a glass-topped tray, and laid it on the counter. The man pored over those tiny vitreous creatures with bright orange feet and belted bodies. Pilgram pointed with the stem of his pipe to one of the rows, and simultaneously the man exclaimed: 'Good God – *uralensis!*' and that ejaculation gave him away. Pilgram heaped case after case on the counter as it dawned upon him that the visitor knew perfectly well of the existence of his collection, had come for its sake, was as a matter of fact the rich amateur Sommer, to whom he had written and who had just returned from a trip to Venezuela; and finally, when the question was carelessly put – 'Well, and what would the price be?' – Pilgram smiled.

He knew it was madness; he knew he was leaving a helpless Eleanor, debts, unpaid taxes, a store at which only trash was bought; he knew that the 950 marks he might get would permit him to travel for no longer than a few months; and still he accepted it all as a man who felt that tomorrow would bring dreary old age and that the good fortune which now beckoned would never again repeat its invitation.

When finally Sommer said that on the fourth he would give a definite answer, Pilgram decided that the dream of his life was about to break at last from its old crinkly cocoon. He spent several hours examining a map, choosing a route, estimating the time of appearance of this or that species, and suddenly something black and blinding welled before his eyes, and he stumbled about his shop for quite a while before he felt better. The fourth came and Sommer failed to turn up, and, after waiting all day, Pilgram retired to his bedroom and silently lay down. He refused his supper, and for several minutes, with his eyes closed, nagged his wife, thinking she was still standing near; then he heard her sobbing softly in the kitchen, and toyed with the idea of taking an axe and splitting her pale-haired head. Next day he stayed in bed, and Eleanor took his place in the shop and sold a box of watercolours. And after still another day, when the whole thing seemed merely delirium, Sommer, a carnation in his buttonhole and his macintosh on his arm, entered the store. And when he took out a wad, and the banknotes rustled, Pilgram's nose began to bleed violently.

The delivery of the cabinet and a visit to the credulous old woman, to whom he reluctantly gave 50 marks, were his last business in town. The much more expensive visit to the travel agency already referred to his new existence, where only butterflies mattered. Eleanor, though not familiar with her husband's transactions, looked happy, feeling that he had made a good profit, but fearing to ask how much. That afternoon a neighbour dropped in to remind them that tomorrow was the wedding of his daughter. So next morning Eleanor busied herself with brightening up her silk dress and pressing her husband's best suit. She would go there about five, she thought, and he would follow later, after closing time. When he looked up at her with a puzzled frown and then flatly refused to go, it did not surprise her, for she had long become used to all sorts of disappointments. 'There might be champagne,' she said, when already standing in the doorway. No answer – only the shuffling of boxes. She looked thoughtfully at the nice clean gloves on her hands, and went out.

Pilgram, having put the more valuable collections in order, looked at his watch and saw it was time to pack: his train left at 8.29. He locked the shop, dragged out of the corridor his father's old chequered suitcase, and packed the hunting implements first: a folding net, killing jars, pillboxes, a lantern for mothing at night on the sierras, and a few packages of pins. As an afterthought he put in a couple of spreading boards and a cork-bottomed box, though in general he intended to keep his captures in papers, as is usually done when going from place to place. Then he took the suitcase into the bedroom and threw in some thick socks and underwear. He added two or three things that might be sold in an extremity, such as, for instance, a silver tumbler and a bronze medal in a velvet case, which had belonged to his father-in-law.

Again he looked at his watch, and then decided it was time to start for the station. 'Eleanor!' he called loudly, getting into his overcoat. As she did not reply, he looked into the kitchen. No, she was not there; and then vaguely he remembered something about a wedding. Hurriedly he got a scrap of paper and scribbled a few words in pencil. He left the note and the keys in a conspicuous place, and with a chill of excitment, a sinking feeling in the pit of the stomach, verified for the last time whether the money and tickets were in his wallet. *'Also los!'* said Pilgram, and gripped the suitcase.

But, as it was his first journey, he still kept worrying nervously whether there was anything he might have forgotten; then it occurred to him that he had no small change, and he remembered the clay money-pot where there might be a few coins. Groaning and knocking the heavy suitcase against corners, he returned to his counter. In the twilight of the strangely still shop, eyed wings stared at him from all sides, and Pilgram perceived something almost appalling in the richness of the huge happiness that was leaning towards him like a mountain. Trying to avoid the knowing looks of those numberless eyes, he drew a deep breath and, catching sight of the hazy money-pot, which seemed to hang in mid-air, reached quickly for it. The pot slipped from his moist grasp and broke on the floor with a dizzy spinning of twinkling coins, and Pilgram bent low to pick them up.

4

Night came; a slippery polished moon sped, without the least friction, in between chinchilla clouds, and Eleanor, returning from the wedding supper, and still all a-tingle from the wine and the juicy jokes, recalled her own wedding day as she leisurely walked home. Somehow all the thoughts now passing through her brain kept turning so as to show their moon-bright, attractive side; she felt almost light-hearted as she entered the gateway and proceeded to open the door, and she caught herself thinking that it was surely a great thing to have an apartment of one's own, stuffy and dark though it might be. Smiling, she turned on the light in her bedroom, and saw at once that all the drawers had been pulled open: she hardly had time to imagine burglars, for there were those keys on the night table and a bit of paper propped against the alarm clock. The note was brief: 'Off to Spain. Don't touch anything till I write. Borrow from Sch. or W. Feed the lizards.'

The tap was dripping in the kitchen. Unconsciously she picked up her silver bag where she had dropped it, and kept on sitting on the edge of the bed, quite straight and still, with her hands in her lap as if she were having her photograph taken. After a time someone got up, walked across the room, inspected the bolted window, came back again, while she watched with indifference, not realizing that it was she who was moving. The drops of water plopped in slow succession, and suddenly she felt terrified at being alone in the house. The man whom she had loved for his mute omniscience, stolid coarseness, grim perseverance in work, had stolen away . . . She felt like howling, running to the police, showing her marriage certificate, insisting, pleading; but still she kept on sitting, her hair slightly ruffled, her hands in white gloves.

Yes, Pilgram had gone far, very far. Most probably he visited Granada and Murcia and Albarracin, and then travelled farther still, to Surinam or Taprobane; and one can hardly doubt that he saw all the glorious bugs he had longed to see – velvety black butterflies soaring over the jungles, and a tiny moth in Tasmania, and that Chinese 'skipper' said to smell of crushed roses when alive, and the short-clubbed beauty that a Mr Baron had just discovered in Mexico. So, in a certain sense, it is quite irrelevant that some time later, upon wandering into the shop, Eleanor saw the chequered suitcase, and then her husband, sprawling on the floor with his back to the counter, among scattered coins, his livid face knocked out of shape by death.

Berlin, 1931

Signs and Symbols

I

For the fourth time in as many years they were confronted with the problem of what birthday present to bring a young man who was incurably deranged in his mind. He had no desires. Man-made objects were to him either hives of evil, vibrant with a malignant activity that he alone could perceive, or gross comforts for which no use could be found in his abstract world. After eliminating a number of articles that might offend him or frighten him (anything in the gadget line for instance was taboo), his parents chose a dainty and innocent trifle: a basket with ten different fruit jellies in ten little jars.

At the time of his birth they had been married already for a long time: a score of years had elapsed, and now they were quite old. Her drab grey hair was done anyhow. She wore cheap black dresses. Unlike other women of her age (such as Mrs Sol, their next-door neighbour, whose face was all pink and mauve with paint and whose hat was a cluster of brookside flowers), she presented a naked white countenance to the fault-finding light of spring days. Her husband, who in the old country had been a fairly successful businessman, was now wholly dependent on his brother Isaac, a real American of almost forty years standing. They seldom saw him and had nicknamed him 'the Prince'.

That Friday everything went wrong. The Underground train lost its life current between two stations, and for a quarter of an hour one could hear nothing but the dutiful beating of one's heart and the rustling of newspapers. The bus they had to take next kept them waiting for ages; and when it did come, it was crammed with garrulous high-school children. It was raining hard as they walked up the brown path leading to the sanitarium. There they waited again; and instead of their boy shuffling into the room as he usually did (his poor face blotched with acne, ill-shaven, sullen, and confused), a nurse they knew, and did not care for, appeared at last and brightly explained that he had again attempted to take his life. He was all right, she said, but a visit might disturb him. The place was so miserably understaffed, and things got mislaid or mixed up so easily, that they decided not to leave their present in the office but to bring it to him next time they came.

She waited for her husband to open his umbrella and

then took his arm. He kept clearing his throat in a special resonant way he had when he was upset. They reached the bus-stop shelter on the other side of the street and he closed his umbrella. A few feet away, under a swaying and dripping tree, a tiny half-dead unfledged bird was helplessly twitching in a puddle.

During the long ride to the Underground station, she and her husband did not exchange a word; and every time she glanced at his old hands (swollen veins, brown-spotted skin), clasped and twitching upon the handle of his umbrella, she felt the mounting pressure of tears. As she looked around trying to hook her mind on to something, it gave her a kind of soft shock, a mixture of compassion and wonder, to notice that one of the passengers, a girl with dark hair and grubby red toenails, was weeping on the shoulder of an older woman. Whom did that woman resemble? She resembled Rebecca Borisovna, whose daughter had married one of the Soloveichiks – in Minsk, years ago.

The last time their son had tried to take his life, his method had been, in the doctor's words, a masterpiece of inventiveness; he would have succeeded, had not an envious fellow patient thought he was learning to fly – and stopped him. What he really wanted to do was to tear a hole in his world and escape.

The system of his delusions had been the subject of

an elaborate paper in a scientific monthly, but long before that she and her husband had puzzled it out for themselves. 'Referential mania', Herman Brink had called it. In these very rare cases the patient imagines that everything happening around him is a veiled reference to his personality and existence. He excludes real people from the conspiracy – because he considers himself to be so much more intelligent than other men. Phenomenal nature shadows him wherever he goes. Clouds in the staring sky transmit to one another, by means of slow signs, incredibly detailed information regarding him. His inmost thoughts are discussed at nightfall, in manual alphabet, by darkly gesticulating trees. Pebbles or stains or sun flecks form patterns representing in some awful way messages which he must intercept. Everything is a cipher and of everything he is the theme. Some of the spies are detached observers, such as glass surfaces and still pools; others, such as coats in store windows, are prejudiced witnesses, lynchers at heart; others again (running water, storms) are hysterical to the point of insanity, have a distorted opinion of him and grotesquely misinterpret his actions. He must be always on his guard and devote every minute and module of life to the decoding of the undulation of things. The very air he exhales is indexed and filed away. If the only interest he provokes were limited to his immediate surroundings – but alas it is not! With distance the torrents of wild scandal increase in volume and volubility. The silhouettes of his blood corpuscles, magnified a million times, flit over vast plains; and still farther, great mountains of unbearable solidity and height sum up in terms of granite and groaning firs the ultimate truth of his being.

2

When they emerged from the thunder and foul air of the Underground railway, the last dregs of the day were mixed with the street lights. She wanted to buy some fish for supper, so she handed him the basket of jelly jars, telling him to go home. He walked up to the third landing and then remembered he had given her the keys earlier in the day.

In silence he sat down on the steps and in silence rose when some ten minutes later she came, heavily trudging upstairs, wanly smiling, shaking her head in deprecation of her silliness. They entered their two-room flat and he at once went to the mirror. Straining the corners of his mouth apart by means of his thumbs, with a horrible mask like grimace, he removed his new hopelessly uncomfortable dental plate and severed the long tusks of saliva connecting him to it. He read his Russian-language newspaper while she laid the table. Still reading, he ate the pale victuals that needed no teeth. She knew his moods and was also silent.

When he had gone to bed, she remained in the living room with her pack of soiled cards and her old albums. Across the narrow yard where the rain tinkled in the dark against some battered ash cans, windows were blandly alight and in one of them a black-trousered man with his bare elbows raised could be seen lying supine on an untidy bed. She pulled the blind down and examined the photographs. As a baby he looked more surprised than most babies. From a fold in the album, a German maid they had in Leipzig and her fat-faced fiancé fell out. Minsk, the Revolution, Leipzig, Berlin, Leipzig, a slanting house front badly out of focus. Four years old, in a park: moodily, shyly, with puckered forehead, looking away from an eager squirrel as he would from any other stranger. Aunt Rosa, a fussy, angular, wild-eyed old lady, who had lived in a tremulous world of bad news, bankruptcies, train accidents, cancerous growths – until the Germans put her to death, together with all the people she had worried about. Aged six – that was when he drew wonderful birds with human hands and feet, and suffered from insomnia like a grown-up man. His cousin, now a famous chess player. He again, aged about eight, already difficult to understand, afraid of the wallpaper in the passage, afraid of a certain picture in a book which merely showed an idyllic landscape with rocks on a hillside and an old cart wheel hanging from the branch of a leafless tree. Aged ten: the year they left Europe. The shame, the pity, the humiliating difficulties, the ugly, vicious, backward children he was with in that special school. And then came a time in his life, coinciding with a long convalescence after pneumonia, when those little phobias of his which his parents had stubbornly regarded as the eccentricities of a prodigiously gifted child hardened as it were into a dense tangle of logically interacting illusions, making him totally inaccessible to normal minds.

This, and much more, she accepted – for after all living did mean accepting the loss of one joy after another, not even joys in her case – mere possibilities of improvement. She thought of the endless waves of pain that for some reason or other she and her husband had to endure; of the invisible giants hurting her boy in some unimaginable fashion; of the incalculable amount of tenderness contained in the world; of the fate of this tenderness, which is either crushed, or wasted, or transformed into madness; of neglected children humming to themselves in unswept corners; of beautiful weeds that cannot hide from the farmer and helplessly have to watch the shadow of his simian stoop leave mangled flowers in its wake, as the monstrous darkness approaches.

3

It was past midnight when from the living room she heard her husband moan; and presently he staggered in, wearing over his nightgown the old overcoat with astrakhan collar which he much preferred to the nice blue bathrobe he had.

'I can't sleep,' he cried.

'Why,' she asked, 'why can't you sleep? You were so tired.'

'I can't sleep because I am dying,' he said and lay down on the couch.

'Is it your stomach? Do you want me to call Dr Solov?'

'No doctors, no doctors,' he moaned: 'To the devil with doctors! We must get him out of there quick. Otherwise we'll be responsible. Responsible!' he repeated and hurled himself into a sitting position, both feet on the floor, thumping his forehead with his clenched fist.

'All right,' she said quietly, 'we shall bring him home tomorrow morning.'

'I would like some tea,' said her husband and retired to the bathroom.

Bending with difficulty, she retrieved some playing

cards and a photograph or two that had slipped from the couch to the floor: knave of hearts, nine of spades, ace of spades. Elsa and her bestial beau.

He returned in high spirits, saying in a loud voice:

'I have it all figured out. We will give him the bedroom. Each of us will spend part of the night near him and the other part on this couch. By turns. We will have the doctor see him at least twice a week. It does not matter what the Prince says. He won't have to say much anyway because it will come out cheaper.'

The telephone rang. It was an unusual hour for their telephone to ring. His left slipper had come off and he groped for it with his heel and toe as he stood in the middle of the room, and childishly, toothlessly, gaped at his wife. Having more English than he did, it was she who attended to calls.

'Can I speak to Charlie,' said a girl's dull little voice.

'What number you want? No. That is not the right number.'

The receiver was gently cradled. Her hand went to her old tired heart.

'It frightened me,' she said.

He smiled a quick smile and immediately resumed his excited monologue. They would fetch him as soon as it was day. Knives would have to be kept in a locked drawer.

Even at his worst he represented no danger to other people.

The telephone rang a second time. The same toneless anxious young voice asked for Charlie.

'You have the incorrect number. I will tell you what you are doing; you are turning the letter O instead of the zero.'

They sat down to their unexpected festive midnight tea. The birthday present stood on the table. He sipped noisily; his face was flushed; every now and then he imparted a circular motion to his raised glass so as to make the sugar dissolve more thoroughly. The vein on the side of his bald head where there was a large birthmark stood out conspicuously and, although he had shaved that morning, a silvery bristle showed on his chin. While she poured him another glass of tea, he put on his spectacles and re-examined with pleasure the luminous yellow, green, red little jars. His clumsy moist lips spelled out their eloquent labels: apricot, grape, beech plum, quince. He had got to crab apple, when the telephone rang again.

Boston, 1948

Lance

I

The name of the planet, presuming it has already received one, is immaterial. At its most favoured opposition, it may very well be separated from the earth by only as many miles as there are years between last Friday and the rise of the Himalayas – a million times the reader's average age. In the telescopic field of one's fancy, through the prism of one's tears, any particularities it presents should be no more striking than those of existing planets. A rosy globe, marbled with dusky blotches, it is one of the countless objects diligently revolving in the infinite and gratuitous awfulness of fluid space.

My planet's *maria* (which are not seas) and its *lacus* (which are not lakes) have also, let us suppose, received names; some less jejune, perhaps, than those of garden roses; others, more pointless than the surnames of their observers (for, to take actual cases, that an astronomer should have been called Lampland is as marvellous as that an entomologist should have been called Kraut-wurm); but most of them of so antique a style as to vie in sonorous and corrupt enchantment with place names pertaining to romances of chivalry.

Just as our Pinedales, down here, have often little to offer beyond a shoe factory on one side of the tracks and the rusty inferno of an automobile dump on the other, so these seductive Arcadias and Icarias and Zephyrias on planetary maps may quite likely turn out to be dead deserts lacking even the milkweed that graces our dumps. Selenographers will confirm this, but then their lenses serve them better than ours do. In the present instance, the greater the magnification, the more the mottling of the planet's surface looks as if it were seen by a submerged swimmer peering up through semi-translucent water. And if certain connected markings resemble in a shadowy way the line-and-hole pattern of a Chinese-checkers board, let us consider them geometrical hallucinations.

I not only debar a too definite planet from any role in my story – from the role every dot and full stop should play in my story (which I see as a kind of celestial chart) – I also refuse to have anything to do with those technical prophecies that scientists are reported to make to reporters. Not for me is the rocket racket. Not for me are the artificial little satellites that the earth is promised;

landing star-strips for spaceships ('spacers') – one, two, three, four, and then thousands of strong castles in the air each complete with cookhouse and keep, set up by terrestrial nations in a frenzy of competitive confusion, phony gravitation, and savagely flapping flags.

Another thing I have not the slightest use for is the special-equipment business – the airtight suit, the oxygen apparatus – suchlike contraptions. Like old Mr Boke, of whom we shall hear in a minute, I am eminently qualified to dismiss these practical matters (which anyway are doomed to seem absurdly impractical to future spaceshipmen, such as old Boke's only son), since the emotions that gadgets provoke in me range from dull distrust to morbid trepidation. Only by a heroic effort can I make myself unscrew a bulb that has died an inexplicable death and screw in another, which will light up in my face with the hideous instancy of a dragon's egg hatching in one's bare hand.

Finally, I utterly spurn and reject so-called 'science fiction'. I have looked into it, and found it as boring as the mystery-story magazines – the same sort of dismally pedestrian writing with oodles of dialogue and loads of commutational humour. The clichés are, of course, disguised; essentially, they are the same throughout all cheap reading matter, whether it spans the universe or the living room. They are like those 'assorted' cookies that differ from one another only in shape and shade, whereby their shrewd makers ensnare the salivating consumer in a mad Pavlovian world where, at no extra cost, variations in simple visual values influence and gradually replace flavour, which thus goes the way of talent and truth.

So the good guy grins, and the villain sneers, and a noble heart sports a slangy speech. Star tsars, directors of Galactic Unions, are practically replicas of those peppy, red-haired executives in earthy earth jobs, that illustrate with their little crinkles the human interest stories of the well-thumbed slicks in beauty parlours. Invaders of Denebola and Spica, Virgo's finest, bear names beginning with Mac; cold scientists are usually found under Steins; some of them share with the super-galactic gals such abstract labels as Biola or Vala. Inhabitants of foreign planets, 'intelligent' beings, humanoid or of various mythic makes, have one remarkable trait in common; their intimate structure is never depicted. In a supreme concession to biped propriety, not only do centaurs wear loincloths; they wear them about their forelegs.

This seems to complete the elimination – unless anybody wants to discuss the question of time? Here again, in order to focalize young Emery L. Boke, that more or less remote descendant of mine who is to be a member of the first interplanetary expedition (which, after all, is the one humble postulate of my tale), I gladly leave the replacement by a pretentious '2' or '3' of the honest '1' in our '1900' to the capable paws of *Starzan* and other comics and atomics. Let it be A.D. or A.A. 200, it does not matter. I have no desire to barge into vested interests of any kind. This is strictly an amateur performance, with quite casual stage properties and a minimum of scenery, and the quilled remains of a dead porcupine in a corner of the old barn. We are here among friends, the Browns and the Bensons, the Whites and the Wilsons, and when somebody goes out for a smoke, he hears the crickets, and a distant farm dog (who waits, between barks, to listen to what we cannot hear). The summer night sky is a mess of stars. Emery Lancelot Boke, at twenty-one, knows immeasurably more about them than I, who am fifty and terrified.

2

Lance is tall and lean, with thick tendons and greenish veins on his sun-tanned forearms and a scar on his brow. When doing nothing – when sitting ill at ease as he sits now, leaning forward from the edge of a low armchair, his shoulders hunched up, his elbows propped on his big knees – he has a way of slowly clasping and unclasping his handsome hands, a gesture I borrow for him from one of his ancestors. An air of gravity, of uncomfortable concentration (all thought is uncomfortable, and young thought especially so), is his usual expression; at the moment, however, it is a manner of mask, concealing his furious desire to get rid of a long-drawn tension. As a rule, he does not smile often, and besides 'smile' is too smooth a word for the abrupt, bright contortion that now suddenly illumines his mouth and eyes as the shoulders hunch higher, the moving hands stop in a clasped position and he lightly stamps the toe of one foot. His parents are in the room, and also a chance visitor, a fool and a bore, who is not aware of what is happening – for this is an awkward moment in a gloomy house on the eve of a fabulous departure.

An hour goes by. At last the visitor picks up his top hat from the carpet and leaves. Lance remains alone with his parents, which only serves to increase the tension. Mr Boke I see plainly enough. But I cannot visualize Mrs Boke with any degree of clarity, no matter how deep I sink into my difficult trance. I know that her cheerfulness – small talk, quick beat of eyelashes – is something she keeps up not so much for the sake of her son as for that of her husband, and his ageing heart, and old Boke realizes this only too well and, on top of his own monstrous anguish, he has to cope with her feigned levity, which disturbs him more than would an utter and unconditional collapse. I am somewhat disappointed that I cannot make out her features. All I manage to glimpse is an effect of melting light on one side of her misty hair, and in this, I suspect, I am insidiously influenced by the standard artistry of modern photography and I feel how much easier writing must have been in former days when one's imagination was not hemmed in by innumerable visual aids, and a frontiersman looking at his first giant cactus or his first high snows was not necessarily reminded of a tyre company's pictorial advertisement.

In the case of Mr Boke, I find myself operating with the features of an old professor of history, a brilliant medievalist, whose white whiskers, pink pate and black suit are famous on a certain sunny campus in the deep South, but whose sole asset in connection with this story (apart from a slight resemblance to a long-dead great-uncle of mine) is that his appearance is out of date. Now if one is perfectly honest with oneself, there is nothing extraordinary in the tendency to give to the manners and clothes of a distant day (which happens to be placed in the future) an old-fashioned tinge, a badly pressed, badly groomed, dusty something, since the terms 'out of date', 'not of our age', and so on are in the long run the only ones in which we are able to imagine and express a strangeness no amount of research can foresee. The future is but the obsolete in reverse.

In that shabby room, in the tawny lamplight, Lance talks of some last things. He has recently brought from a desolate spot in the Andes, where he has been climbing some as yet unnamed peak, a couple of adolescent chinchillas – cinder-grey, phenomenally furry, rabbit-sized rodents (*Hystricomorpha*), with long whiskers, round rumps and petal-like ears. He keeps them indoors in a wire-screened pen and gives them peanuts, puffed rice, raisins to eat, and, as a special treat, a violet or an aster. He hopes they will breed in the fall. He now repeats to his mother a few emphatic instructions – to keep his pets' food crisp and their pen dry, and never forget their daily dust bath (fine sand mixed with powdered chalk) in which they roll and kick most lustily. While this is being discussed, Mr Boke lights and re-lights a pipe and finally puts it away. Every now and then, with a false air of benevolent absent-mindedness, the old man launches upon a series of sounds and motions that deceive nobody; he clears his throat and, with his hands behind his back, drifts towards a window; or he begins to produce a tight-lipped tuneless humming; and seemingly driven by that small nasal motor, he wanders out of the parlour. But no sooner has he left the stage than he throws off, with a dreadful shiver, the elaborate structure of his gentle, bumbling impersonation act. In a bedroom or bathroom, he stops as if to take, in abject solitude, a deep spasmodic draught from some secret flask, and presently staggers out again, drunk with grief.

The stage has not changed when he quietly returns to it, buttoning his coat and resuming that little hum. It is now a matter of minutes. Lance inspects the pen before he goes, and leaves Chin and Chilla sitting on their haunches, each holding a flower. The only other thing that I know about these last moments is that any such talk as 'Sure you haven't forgotten the silk shirt that came from the wash?' or 'You remember where you put those new slippers?' is excluded. Whatever Lance takes with him is already collected at the mysterious and unmentionable and absolutely awful place of his zero-hour departure; he needs nothing of what we need; and he steps out of the house, empty-handed and hatless, with the casual lightness of one walking to the news-stand – or to a glorious scaffold.

3

Terrestrial space loves concealment. The most it yields to the eye is a panoramic view. The horizon closes upon the receding traveller like a trapdoor in slow motion. For those who remain, any town a day's journey from

here is invisible, whereas you can easily see such trans-
cendencies as, say, a lunar amphitheatre and the shadow
cast by its circular ridge. The conjurer who displays the
firmament has rolled up his sleeves and performs in full
view of the little spectators. Planets may dip out of sight
(just as objects are obliterated by the blurry curve of
one's own cheekbone); but they are back when the earth
turns its head. The nakedness of the night is appalling.
Lance has left; the fragility of his young limbs grows in
direct ratio to the distance he covers. From their balcony,
the old Bokes look at the infinitely perilous night sky and
wildly envy the lot of fishermen's wives.

If Boke's sources are accurate, the name 'Lanceloz del
Lac' occurs for the first time in Verse 3676 of the twelfth-
century *Roman de la Charrette*. Lance, Lancelin, Lancelotik –
diminutives murmured at the brimming, salty, moist
stars. Young knights in their teens learning to harp,
hawk and hunt; the Forest Dangerous and the Dolorous
Tower; Aldebaran, Betelgeuse – the thunder of Sarace-
nic war cries. Marvellous deeds of arms, marvellous
warriors, sparkling within the awful constellations
above the Bokes' balcony: Sir Percard the Black Knight,
and Sir Perimones the Red Knight, and Sir Pertolepe the
Green Knight, and Sir Persant the Indigo Knight, and
that bluff old party Sir Grummore Grummursum, muttering northern oaths under his breath. The field glass is

not much good, the chart is all crumpled and damp, and: 'You do not hold the flashlight properly' – this to Mrs Boke.

Draw a deep breath. Look again.

Lancelot is gone; the hope of seeing him in life is about equal to the hope of seeing him in eternity. Lancelot is banished from the country of L'Eau Grise (as we might call the Great Lakes) and now rides up in the dust of the night sky almost as fast as our local universe (with the balcony and the pitch-black, optically spotted garden) speeds towards King Arthur's Harp, where Vega burns and beckons – one of the few objects that can be identified by the aid of this goddam diagram. The sidereal haze makes the Bokes dizzy – grey incense, insanity, infinity-sickness. But they cannot tear themselves away from the nightmare of space, cannot go back to the lighted bedroom, a corner of which shows in the glass door. And presently *the* planet rises, like a tiny bonfire.

There, to the right, is the Bridge of the Sword leading to the Otherworld (*'dont nus estranges ne retorne'*). Lancelot crawls over it in great pain, in ineffable anguish. 'Thou shalt not pass a pass that is called the Pass Perilous.' But another enchanter commands: 'You shall. You shall even acquire a sense of humour that will tide you over the trying spots.' The brave old Bokes think they can distinguish Lance scaling, on crampons, the

verglassed rock of the sky or silently breaking trail
through the soft snows of nebulae. Boötes, somewhere
between camp X and XI, is a great glacier all rubble and
icefall. We try to make out the serpentine route of
ascent; seem to distinguish the light leanness of Lance
among the several roped silhouettes. Gone! Was it he or
Denny (a young biologist, Lance's best friend)? Waiting
in the dark valley at the foot of the vertical sky, we recall
(Mrs Boke more clearly than her husband) those special
names for crevasses and Gothic structures of ice that
Lance used to mouth with such professional gusto in his
alpine boyhood (he is several light-years older by now);
the séracs and the schrunds; the avalanche and its thud;
French echoes and Germanic magic hobnailnobbing up
there as they do in medieval romances.

Ah, there he is again! Crossing through a notch
between two stars; then, very slowly, attempting a trav-
erse on a cliff face so sheer, and with such delicate holds
that the mere evocation of those groping fingertips and
scraping boots filled one with acrophobic nausea. And
through streaming tears the old Bokes see Lance now
marooned on a shelf of stone and now climbing again
and now, dreadfully safe, with his ice axe and pack, on a
peak above peaks, his eager profile rimmed with light.

Or is he already on his way down? I assume that no
news comes from the explorers and that the Bokes

prolong their pathetic vigils. As they wait for their son to return, his every avenue of descent seems to run into the precipice of their despair. But perhaps he has swung over those high-angled wet slabs that fall away vertically into the abyss, has mastered the overhang, and is now blissfully glissading down steep celestial snows?

As, however, the Bokes' doorbell does not ring at the logical culmination of an imagined series of footfalls (no matter how patiently we space them as they come nearer and nearer in our mind), we have to thrust him back and have him start his ascent all over again, and then put him even farther back, so that he is still at headquarters (where the tents are, and the open latrines, and the begging, black-footed children) long after we had pictured him bending under the tulip tree to walk up the lawn to the door and the doorbell. As if tired by the many appearances he has made in his parents' minds, Lance now ploughs wearily through mud puddles, then up a hillside, in the haggard landscape of a distant war, slipping and scrambling up the dead grass of the slope. There is some routine rock-work ahead, and then the summit. The ridge is won. Our losses are heavy. How is one notified? By wire? By registered letter? And who is the executioner – a special messenger or the regular plodding, florid-nosed postman, always a little high (he has troubles of his own)? Sign here. Big thumb. Small

cross. Weak pencil. Its dull-violet wood. Return it. The
illegible signature of teetering disaster.

But nothing comes. A month passes. Chin and Chilla
are in fine shape and seem very fond of each other –
sleep together in the nestbox, cuddled up in a fluffy ball.
After many tries, Lance has discovered a sound with definite chinchillan appeal, produced by pursing the lips and
emitting in rapid succession several soft, moist 'surpths',
as if taking sips from a straw when most of one's drink
is finished and only its dregs are drained. But his parents
cannot produce it – the pitch is wrong or something.
And there is such an intolerable silence in Lance's room,
with its battered books, and the spotty white shelves, and
the old shoes, and the relatively new tennis racket in its
preposterously secure press, and a penny on the closet
floor – and all this begins to undergo a prismatic dissolu-
tion, but then you tighten the screw and everything is
again in focus. And presently the Bokes return to their
balcony. Has he reached his goal – and if so, does he
see us?

4

The classical ex-mortal leans on his elbow from a flow-
ered ledge to contemplate this earth, this toy, this teeto-
tum gyrating on slow display in its model firmament,

every feature so gay and clear – the painted oceans, and the praying woman of the Baltic, and a still of the elegant Americas caught in their trapeze act, and Australia like a baby Africa lying on its side. There may be people among my coevals who half expect their spirits to look down from Heaven with a shudder and a sigh at their native planet and see it girdled with latitudes, stayed with meridians, and marked, perhaps, with the fat, black, diabolically curving arrows of global wars; or, more pleasantly, spread out before their gaze like one of those picture maps of vacational Eldorados, with a reservation Indian beating a drum here, a girl clad in shorts there, conical conifers, climbing the cones of mountains, and anglers all over the place.

Actually, I suppose, my young descendant on his first night out, in the imagined silence of an unimaginable world, would have to view the surface features of our globe through the depths of its atmosphere; this would mean dust, scattered reflections, haze, and all kinds of optical pitfalls, so that continents, if they appeared at all through the varying clouds, would slip by in queer disguises, with inexplicable gleams of colour and unrecognizable outlines.

But all this is a minor point. The main problem is: Will the mind of the explorer survive the shock? One tries to perceive the nature of that shock as plainly as mental safety permits. And if the mere act of imagining the matter is fraught with hideous risks, how, then, will the real pang be endured and overcome?

First of all, Lance will have to deal with the atavistic moment. Myths have become so firmly entrenched in the radiant sky that common sense is apt to shirk the task of getting at the uncommon sense behind them. Immortality must have a star to stand on if it wishes to branch and blossom and support thousands of blue-plumed angel birds all singing as sweetly as little eunuchs. Deep in the human mind, the concept of dying is synonymous with that of leaving the earth. To escape its gravity means to transcend the grave, and a man upon finding himself on another planet has really no way of proving to himself that he is not dead – that the naïve old myth has not come true.

I am not concerned with the moron, the ordinary hairless ape, who takes everything in his stride; his only childhood memory is of a mule that bit him: his only consciousness of the future a vision of board and bed. What I am thinking of is the man of imagination and science, whose courage is infinite because his curiosity surpasses his courage. Nothing will keep him back. He is the ancient *curieux*, but of a hardier build, with a ruddier heart. When it comes to exploring a celestial body, his is the satisfaction of a passionate desire to feel with his own fingers, to stroke and inspect, and smile at, and inhale, and stroke again – with that same smile of nameless, moaning, melting pleasure – the never-before-touched matter of which the celestial object is made. Any true scientist (not, of course, the fraudulent mediocrity, whose only treasure is the ignorance he hides like a bone) should be capable of experiencing that sensuous pleasure of direct and divine knowledge. He may be twenty or he may be eighty-five but without that tingle there is no science. And of that stuff Lance is made.

Straining my fancy to the utmost, I see him surmounting the panic that the ape might not experience at all. No doubt Lance may have landed in an orange-coloured dust cloud somewhere in the middle of the Tharsis desert (if it is a desert) or near some purple pool – Phoenicis or Oti (if these are lakes after all). But on the other hand . . . You see, as things go in such matters, something is sure to be solved at once, terribly and irrevocably, while other things come up one by one and are puzzled out gradually. When I was a boy . . .

When I was a boy of seven or eight, I used to dream a vaguely recurrent dream set in a certain environment, which I have never been able to recognize and identify in any rational manner, though I have seen many strange lands. I am inclined to make it serve now, in order to patch up a gaping hole, a raw wound in my story. There was nothing spectacular about that environment, nothing monstrous or even odd; just a bit of noncommittal stability represented by a bit of level ground and filmed over with a bit of neutral nebulosity; in other words, the indifferent back of a view rather than its face – the nuisance of that dream was that for some reason I could not walk *around* the view to meet it on equal terms. There lurked in the mist a mass of something – mineral matter or the like – oppressively and quite meaninglessly shaped, and, in the course of my dream, I kept filling some kind of receptacle (translated as 'pail') with smaller shapes (translated as 'pebbles'), and my nose was bleeding but I was too impatient and excited to do anything about it. And every time I had that dream, suddenly somebody would start screaming behind me, and I awoke screaming too, thus prolonging the initial anonymous shriek, with its initial note of rising exultation, but with no meaning attached to it any more – if there *had* been a meaning. Speaking of Lance, I would like to submit that something on the lines of my dream – But the funny thing is that as I reread what I have set down, its background, the factual memory vanishes – has vanished altogether by now – and I have no means of proving to myself that there is any personal experience behind its description. What I wanted to say was that perhaps Lance and his companions, when they reached their planet, felt something akin to my dream – which is no longer mine.

5

And they were back! A horseman, clappity-clap, gallops up the cobbled street to the Bokes' house through the driving rain and shouts out the tremendous news as he stops short at the gate, near the dripping liriodendron, while the Bokes come tearing out of the house like two hystricomorphic rodents. They are back! The pilots, and the astrophysicists, and one of the naturalists, are back (the other, Denny, is dead and has been left in Heaven, the old myth scoring a curious point there).

On the sixth floor of a provincial hospital, carefully hidden from newspapermen, Mr and Mrs Boke are told that their boy is in a little waiting room, second to the right, ready to receive them; there is something, a kind of hushed deference about the tone of this information, as if it referred to a fairy-tale king. They will enter quietly; a nurse, a Mrs Coover, will be there all the time. Oh, he's all right, they are told – can go home next week, as a matter of fact. However, they should not stay more than a couple of minutes, and no questions, please – just chat about something or other. *You* know. And then say you will be coming again tomorrow or the day after tomorrow.

Lance, grey-robed, crop-haired, tan gone, changed, unchanged, changed, thin, nostrils stopped with absorbent cotton, sits on the edge of a couch, his hands clasped, a little embarrassed. Gets up wavily, with a beaming grimace, and sits down again. Mrs Coover, the nurse, has blue eyes and no chin.

A ripe silence. Then Lance: 'It was wonderful. Perfectly wonderful. I am going back in November.'

Pause.

'I think,' says Mr Boke, 'that Chilla is with child.'

Quick smile, little bow of pleased acknowledgement. Then, in a narrative voice: *'Je vais dire ça en français. Nous venions d'arriver —'*

'Show them the President's letter,' says Mrs Coover.

'We had just got there,' Lance continues, 'and Denny was still alive, and the first thing he and I saw —'

In a sudden flutter, Nurse Coover interrupts: 'No, Lance, no. No, Madam, please. No contacts, doctor's orders, *please.*'

Warm temple, cold ear.

Mr and Mrs Boke are ushered out. They walk swiftly — although there is no hurry, no hurry whatever, down the corridor, along its shoddy, olive-and-ochre wall, down the lower olive separated from the upper ochre by a continuous brown line leading to the venerable elevators. Going up (glimpse of patriarch in wheelchair). Going back in November (Lancelin). Going down (the old Bokes). There are, in that elevator, two smiling women and, the object of their bright sympathy, a girl with a baby, besides the grey-haired, bent, sullen elevator man, who stands with his back to everybody.

Ithaca, 1952